Don't miss any of the cases in the Hardy Boys Clue Book series!

THE GREAT PUMPKIN SMAS

HARDY BOYS

→ Clue Book ←

#10

THE GREAT PUMPKIN SMASH

BY FRANKLIN W. DIXON ⇆ ILLUSTRATED BY SANTY GUTIÉRREZ

ALADDIN

NEW YORK   LONDON   TORONTO   SYDNEY   NEW DELHI

ALADDIN

An imprint of Simon & Schuster Children's Publishing Division
1230 Avenue of the Americas, New York, NY 10020
First Aladdin hardcover edition September 2019
Text copyright © 2019 by Simon & Schuster, Inc.
Illustrations copyright © 2019 by Santy Gutiérrez
Also available in an Aladdin paperback edition.

For information about special discounts for bulk purchases, please contact
Simon & Schuster Special Sales at 1-866-506-1949 or business@simonandschuster.com.
The Simon & Schuster Speakers Bureau can bring authors to your live event.
For more information or to book an event contact the Simon & Schuster Speakers Bureau
at 1-866-248-3049 or visit our website at www.simonspeakers.com.
Series designed by Karina Granda
Jacket designed by Tiara Iandiorio
The text of this book was set in Adobe Garamond Pro.
Manufactured in the United States of America 0719 FFG
2 4 6 8 10 9 7 5 3 1
Library of Congress Cataloging-in-Publication Data
Names: Dixon, Franklin W., author. | Gutiérrez, Santy, 1971- illustrator.
Title: The great pumpkin smash / by Franklin W. Dixon ; illustrated by Santy Gutierrez.
Description: First Aladdin hardcover/paperback edition. | New York : Aladdin, 2019. | Series:
Hardy boys clue book ; #10 | Summary: Brothers Frank and Joe Hardy investigate strange
occurrences during Bayport Zoo's annual Halloween party, Boo at the Zoo.
Identifiers: LCCN 2018046689 (print) | LCCN 2018051577 (eBook) |
ISBN 9781534431256 (eBook) | ISBN 9781534431232 (pbk) | ISBN 9781534431249 (hc)
Subjects: | CYAC: Zoos—Fiction. | Halloween—Fiction. |
Brothers—Fiction. | Mystery and detective stories.
Classification: LCC PZ7.D644 (eBook) | LCC PZ7.D644 Gv 2019 (print) |
DDC [Fic]—dc23
LC record available at https://lccn.loc.gov/2018046689

CONTENTS

Chapter

1

BOO CREW

"Hey, Joe. Since when does the Frankenstein monster carry a clue book?" nine-year-old Frank Hardy asked his brother.

Joe smiled as he patted the book in the pocket of his monster costume. "When it's a boo book!" he joked.

Their best friend, Chet Morton, groaned at Joe's joke. He knew the brothers loved solving mysteries more than anything. But that Saturday even the best kid detectives in Bayport had other plans. Every kid in town was dressed in Halloween costumes to rock Boo at the Zoo, Bayport Zoo's annual Halloween party.

Frank was dressed up as Dr. Frankenstein, Joe was the Frankenstein monster, and Chet looked like a giant squeeze bottle of ketchup.

Joe pointed to the can in Chet's hand. "Why did you bring whipped cream, Chet?" he asked. "Won't there be enough stuff to eat at the trick-or-treat stations?"

"I'm in the pumpkin-pie-eating contest," Chet said. "In case they forgot the whipped cream—I brought my own!"

Frank and Joe wished they could watch their serious-snacking friend in the pumpkin-pie-eating contest. But at the same time was another contest the brothers were psyched about.

"Did you memorize our song for the Scaryoke contest, Joe?" Frank asked.

"Are you kidding?" said Joe with a grin. "I know our song so well it's scary!"

"As scary as the Haunted Woods?" Chet teased.

Joe gulped. Each year a Haunted Woods filled with all kinds of creepy stuff was set up inside the zoo's park. And each year Joe refused to go in!

"Um—here comes Aunt Trudy!" Joe said, happy to change the subject. The brothers' aunt had brought them and Chet to the zoo. She had also come on her own mission. . . .

"I found the zoo's schedule of events, boys," said Aunt Trudy, hurrying over. "Just as I thought, there are no activities for the animals today!"

Aunt Trudy pointed to the schedule. "It's time animals had fun on Halloween too, and I'm going to make sure they do!"

"How?" Chet asked.

"That's exactly why I'm here, Chet," Aunt Trudy said, and popped a safari hat on her head. "Now if you boys will excuse me, I'm off on a fact-finding safari."

After handing Frank a copy of the schedule and planning for the boys to check in with her from time to time, Aunt Trudy headed off.

"Is your aunt always on some kind of mission?" Chet asked.

"Only when it comes to animals," said Frank.

Joe looked up at a banner hanging from a lamppost. "Well, we're on our own mission, you guys," he said. "To see him!"

"Him" was the boys' favorite strongman, Victor the Constrictor, who they had seen in several TV appearances. On the banner, the hulk's upper body was tattooed with scales and bulging with muscles. He wore his famous cobra headpiece and reptilian-claw gloves. Between the massive claws was a watermelon about to be smashed to "slither-eens"!

"Awesome!" Chet said, gazing up at Victor's image. "You can almost hear him hiss."

Frank looked at the schedule of the events at the Boo.

"Victor's show is at eleven o'clock, right before the pumpkin pie and Scaryoke contests," he said. "It says he'll be smashing a whole pumpkin. Do you think he can do it?"

"Victor once smashed a bowling ball between his hands," Joe scoffed. "Pumpkins are pistachio nuts to him!"

"Never drop pistachio nut shells on the ground," a voice piped up. "They're poorly digested by juvenile squirrels."

"Huh?" Joe asked. *Who said that?*

Frank, Joe, and Chet turned to see a boy and a girl, both around their age. They were wearing zookeeper uniforms, hats, and name badges that read BRETT and ELENA.

"Neat!" Chet said. "Are you dressed up as zookeepers for Halloween?"

Brett and Elena rolled their eyes at the question.

"We didn't spend three weeks at Junior Zookeeper Camp this summer to wear Halloween costumes!" Brett sounded insulted.

"Junior zookeepers?" Frank repeated.

Elena nodded proudly. "All junior zookeepers get to work at the Boo this year," she said. "Brett and I are helping with the turtles. That's because we know everything about animals."

"Oh yeah?" asked Chet with a gleam in his eye. "Then why don't elephants use computers?"

Brett and Elena stared at Chet, not answering.

"Because they're afraid of the mouse!" Chet laughed. "Get it—afraid of the mouse!"

"Ha-ha," Joe laughed. "Good one, Chet!"

Brett and Elena were not amused.

"Animal jokes are dumb," Brett muttered as the two walked away.

"I love animal jokes, dude," Joe told Chet.

Frank turned over the schedule to find a map of the zoo. The map showed exhibits like the Primate House, the Sea Lion Sound, and the Big Cat Habitat, all set up in a circle. In the middle was the Boo Petting Zoo and something called the Boo-seum of Pumpkin Arts.

"What do you think that is?" said Frank.

"There's only one way to find out," Joe said. He waved his hand in the direction of the festivities. "Let's check out this Boo and see what's new!"

Chapter 2

TEMPER TENT-RUM

Frank, Joe, and Chet used the map to find the Boo-seum of Pumpkin Arts. It turned out to be a big white tent just a few feet away from the petting zoo.

"Let's see what's inside," Joe suggested. "Last one in is a rotten jack-o'-lantern!"

The three boys filed through the opening. As they looked around, Joe cried, "Cool!"

Spread out over the sawdust-covered ground were about a dozen painted pumpkins. There were pumpkins painted with animal faces, favorite cartoon characters, and splashy designs. A bunch of kids were milling around, checking out the pumpkins.

But one work of art was different from all the rest. In the middle of the tent was a tall pumpkin sculpture put together to look like a giant grasshopper. Next to it stood the boys' schoolmate Oliver Splathall.

Oliver was a famous kid sculptor in Bayport. But as the boys approached him, he was not talking to a fan. He was arguing with a woman wearing pumpkin earrings and an orange pantsuit.

"You're in charge of the contest, Ms. Mitchell," Oliver was saying. "Isn't there anything you can do?"

"I'm sorry, Oliver," Ms. Mitchell said. "This is a pumpkin-painting contest, and your artwork is clearly a sculpture."

"I painted the eyeballs!" Oliver blurted, pointing to the grasshopper's face. "See?"

"I'm afraid two black dots are not enough," Ms. Mitchell said. "Zoo Director Doug told me to stick to the rules."

As Oliver stormed out of the tent, Frank and Joe could hear him mutter, "Rules, schmules. I'll show them!"

Frank and Joe didn't know what Oliver meant by that. All they knew was that he had left his sculpture and tool bag inside the tent.

"Will Oliver be okay?" a girl asked.

"Yes," Ms. Mitchell said with a small smile. "He just has an artistic temperament."

"If Oliver has a temperature," a boy said, "he should go home!"

Ms. Mitchell made an announcement for everyone to leave the tent. "It's fifteen minutes before eleven now," she told the kids. "I'm sure you all want to see the Victor the Constrictor Show. Just be sure you're back at noon for the judging."

"What about all these pumpkins?" asked Joe.

"They'll be fine here in the Boo-seum," Ms. Mitchell said. "The tent will be closed until the judging."

Frank, Joe, and Chet left with the others. Ms. Mitchell closed the tent flap and tied it shut.

As they walked away from the tent, Joe said, "I liked Oliver's grasshopper sculpture best."

"Speaking of grasshoppers," said Chet excitedly, "I heard they're giving out gummy bugs in front of the Insect House."

"You're going to eat candy before the pumpkin-pie-eating contest?" Frank asked.

"It's my way of warming up," Chet said with a shrug. "Even athletes do jumping jacks before a big game."

Chet left for the Insect House. Frank and Joe were about to check out the carnival rides when they heard a loud—

"Ee-haw, ee-haw, ee-haw!"

The brothers followed the sound to the petting zoo—a large, fenced-in area. Inside the pen was a braying donkey. There were also other small animals and two junior zookeepers.

Frank reached over the fence to pet a goat. But as Joe coaxed a llama over, Frank said, "Bad idea!"

"Why?" Joe asked as the llama got closer and closer.

"Because," Frank said, "llamas spit!"

The brothers took a step back, but—too late!
With a noisy hock, the llama blew a torpedo of spit
straight at Frank!

"Arrrghhh!" Frank cried as the spit glob landed
square on his chest. "Loogies!"

The junior zookeepers raced over to the fence. The names on their badges read MANUEL and STEPHANIE.

"Okay, okay, what's the problem?" Manuel demanded.

"Your llama spit all over my Dr. Frankenstein lab coat," Frank sighed.

"Now it's a raincoat," Joe joked.

The junior zookeepers remained stone-faced.

"Llamas spit when they're distressed," Stephanie blurted. "What did you say to him?"

"Say to him?" cried Frank.

"Junior zookeepers know how to talk to animals," Manuel stated. "Oh, but you're not junior zoo-keepers, are you?"

Hoping to lighten things up, Joe told the junior zookeepers about the upcoming show. "We're going to see Victor the Constrictor. Are you guys going too?"

"Can't," Manuel said. "We've got a job to do. Right, JZ Squad?"

"Right, JZ Squad!" Stephanie replied.

"You guys must work hard," Frank admitted. "Do you feed all these animals?"

"You bet," Manuel said. "But only special food pellets from the zoo's nutritional compound."

He held out his hand. In his palm was a small hard brown nugget. "This is what the llama eats every day."

Joe wrinkled his nose at the pellet. "Glad I'm not a llama," he said.

"We wash the petting zoo animals too," Stephanie said. "Today we bathed all of them before the zoo opened."

Suddenly Frank and Joe heard a familiar voice. . . .

"A petting zoo!" Aunt Trudy cried, racing toward the pen. She smiled at the junior zookeepers. "How would your animals like to bob for apples? Or if you have a monkey—bananas?"

"Maybe we'd better go," Frank whispered to Joe.

After a quick check-in with Aunt Trudy, the brothers headed for the stage where the Victor the Constrictor Show would be.

"I totally want to wash off this llama spit," Frank said.

"There's no time, Frank," said Joe as he looked at his watch. "The Victor the Constrictor Show starts at eleven, and we want to get good seats."

Frank and Joe picked up their pace—until three tall figures stepped in their way.

"Where do you think you're going?" one growled.

Both brothers gulped. Looming over them were three zombies, looking totally creepy—and real!

SQUEEZY DOES IT!

"I said, where are you going?" the tallest of the zombies demanded.

Frank rolled his eyes. He and Joe would know the voice anywhere. It was Adam Ackerman, Bayport Elementary School's number one bully. The brothers took a wild guess that the other zombies were Adam's equally bully-ish friends, Seth and Tony.

"Hey, Adam," Joe muttered.

Adam sniffed the air. "I thought this was Boo at the Zoo," he said, "Not pe-ew at the zoo."

"And I thought the rules said no super-scary costumes," said Frank, pointing to their zombie suits and makeup.

"If anyone is scared of zombies, that's their problem," Adam scoffed. "Nothing scares us."

"Except snakes," Seth chuckled. "You should see Adam when he sees a snake!"

"That's why Adam doesn't want to see Victor the Constrictor," Tony said with a grin. "He even—"

"Shut up!" Adam snapped, then added, "Let's go. We've got that thing to do."

Frank and Joe were glad to see the bullies leave.

"What do you think 'that thing' is?" Joe asked.

Frank frowned. "What else could it be with Adam and his friends?" he said. "More trouble!"

The brothers followed a crowd of excited kids to the stage. Zoo workers handed out free rubber snake wristbands in honor of the hero, Victor the Constrictor!

Frank and Joe put on their snake bands and found two open spots on a bench to watch the show. On the stage was a big orange pumpkin set up on a stool.

"That must be the pumpkin Victor the Constrictor is going to smash," Frank said.

"To slither-eens, Frank," Joe added excitedly. "To slither-eens!"

Excited whispers filled the air as Bayport Zoo

director Doug Navarro walked onto the stage. Many of the kids chuckled at his Halloween costume—a penguin suit!

Joe leaned forward in his seat. It was showtime!

Director Doug smiled beneath the beak on his hood and boomed, "Welcome to Boo at the Zoo! Now please welcome your favorite snake-skinned star—Victor the Constrictor!!!"

The crowd went wild as Victor slithered across the stage in his scaly costume. Hissing at the audience, he stood up and flexed his muscles.

"You call that a pumpkin?" Victor yelled, pointing to the pumpkin on the stool. "I call it my main squeeze. So what am I going to smash it to, kids?"

"Slither-eens!" Frank, Joe, and the others yelled.

Victor grabbed the pumpkin between his claw-gloved hands. The Hardys watched wide-eyed as he began to hiss and squeeze. A hush fell over the crowd as Victor's biceps bulged, his face reddened, and his teeth gnashed. The constrictor-man seemed to squeeze with all his might, but the pumpkin wouldn't even crack!

"It never takes this long for Victor to smash anything," Joe whispered.

Frank didn't get it either. Especially as Victor's snaky hisses turned into pained grunts. After five whole minutes he slumped over exhausted, dropping the pumpkin back on the stool.

Frank and Joe just groaned with disappointment,

but some kids in the audience really let their frustration be known.

"Some strongman!" one boy shouted. "He probably can't squeeze a tube of toothpaste!"

"He's not a snake," a girl yelled out. "More of a—fake!"

Victor narrowed his eyes at the audience. "So you think I'm a fake, huh?" he demanded. "I may not have squeezed that pumpkin, but I'll show you soon who's the champ!"

He wiggled his tongue like a snake at the audience before stomping off the stage.

Waddling in his penguin suit, Director Doug returned to the mike. "All right, then!" he said with a forced smile. "I guess Victor the Constrictor was just a little . . . viped out!"

"Was that a joke?" Joe whispered to Frank.

"But the fun hasn't ended, kids," Director Doug said. "Because now it's time for . . . Scaryoke!"

A zookeeper dressed as a witch wheeled a giant cauldron onto the stage. The cauldron contained the names of the kids who'd entered the Scaryoke contest.

"Our names are in there, Frank!" Joe said excitedly. "I hope we go first."

The witch cackled as she stirred the cauldron with a long staff. Director Doug reached into the cauldron and pulled out a card. After reading it, he announced, "No bones about it, our first act is about to rock it out. Pelvis Bonesly—come on up!"

A kid wearing a skeleton costume ran onto the stage. His music played as he broke into a number called "Boo Suede Shoes."

After his song, Pelvis spoke into the microphone, "Thank you very much . . . and look out for my new song, 'Are You Bone-some Tonight?'"

Pelvis left the stage to polite applause. Frank and Joe held their breath as the witch stirred the cauldron a second time. Director Doug pulled out the next card and announced, "It's alive! It's alive! Dr. Frankenstein and his monster, come on up!"

"Woo-hoo!" Joe shouted. "That's us!"

In a flash the brothers were onstage, performing their Scaryoke song, "Monster Mash." Joe had a blast singing and lumbering across the stage like Frankenstein's monster. But as he gazed into the audience to see their reaction, he spotted three kids running in the distance. Each one had a long object resting on his shoulder. Joe squinted for a closer look and saw who they were: Adam, Seth, and Tony, the zombies!

Where are they going? Joe thought. *What's that thing they're carrying?*

"Joe!" Frank whispered. "Why did you stop singing and walking like Frankenstein's monster?"

Joe gulped as their music stopped. He pointed to the stick-on bolts on his skull cap, joking into the microphone, "Sorry, guys. Must be a screw loose!"

"Thank you, Dr. Frankenstein and his monster!" Director Doug said, whisking them off the stage. "I'm sure everyone got a—charge—out of that number!"

As they walked away from the stage, Frank asked, "What was up with that, Joe? We rehearsed our song for two weeks!"

"I saw something," Joe explained. "Adam, Seth, and Tony were running with these things on their shoulders."

"What things?" Frank asked.

"I don't know," Joe said. "They were too far away for me to see."

"Forget about those bullies," Frank said. "Do you want to stick around and see who wins the Scaryoke contest?"

"It won't be us, that's for sure," Joe sighed. "Let's see who wins the pumpkin-painting contest instead."

The brothers walked through the festivities to the Boo-seum. The tent flap was open, so they went inside. But as they looked at the pumpkins, they couldn't believe their eyes. . . .

"Holy cannoli!" Joe cried. "Those painted pumpkins are squashed!"

Chapter 4

SMASH-O'-LANTERNS

Frank and Joe stared at all the smashed pump-kins, their shells scattered across the ground. Kids stood over their broken pumpkins, sadly shaking their heads.

"Who would do such a horrible thing?" one girl asked.

"My painted pumpkin!" a boy exclaimed. "It's pulverized!"

Then Director Doug burst into the tent. "I left

the Scaryoke contest as soon as I heard what happened!" he told Ms. Mitchell. When he saw the smashed pumpkins, he cried, "What happened?"

"I arrived back at the tent a little before noon," Ms. Mitchell explained. "The flap I tied shut had been opened. Someone got in!"

"You mean someone broke in!" Director Doug groaned.

"I can't believe it," Ms. Mitchell said, shaking her head. "Something like this has never happened at a Boo at the Zoo!"

"And it never will again!" Doug declared. "I know I'm dressed like a goofy penguin, but I'm dead serious. If the pumpkin-smashing vandals don't come forward by the end of the day, there will be no more Boo at the Zoo—ever!"

Gasps filled the tent.

"No more Boo at the Zoo?" Joe whispered to Frank. "Halloween without the Boo would be like hot cocoa without the marshmallows—right, Frank? . . . Frank?"

Frank was too busy staring at Oliver's grasshopper

sculpture to answer. "Check it out, Joe," he said. "The only pumpkins not smashed were the ones on Oliver's sculpture. They haven't been touched."

"Not only that," Joe pointed out. "The tool bag Oliver left behind isn't here anymore."

Before Frank and Joe could get a better look, Ms. Mitchell announced, "Everyone clear the Boo-seum, please, so Mr. Navarro and I can discuss the next steps."

"I know our next step," Frank said as he and Joe left the tent with the others. "To find the pumpkin smasher and save the Boo at the Zoo!"

"In that case," Joe said with a smile, "it's a good thing I brought this!"

Joe pulled out their clue book and pencil, and turned to a fresh page. "Okay. Where do we start?"

"Where detectives like us usually start," said Frank. "With the five *W*s: *who*, *what*, *where*, *when*, and *why*."

"How come the five *W*s start with *who*?" Joe asked. "If we knew who smashed the pumpkins, we wouldn't have a case!"

THE FIVE W's
1. Who ???
2. What *the pumpkins were pulverized*
3. Where *inside the Boo-seum*
4. When *between 11:00 & Noon*?
5. Why?

Joe decided to start with *what* and *where*. Those were the easiest *W*s so far. . . .

"What happened was that the painted pumpkins were pulverized," he said as he wrote. "The *where* was inside the Boo-seum."

"When did it happen?" Frank wondered out loud.

"That's the tricky part," Joe admitted.

"When Ms. Mitchell closed the tent, it was a little before eleven o'clock," Frank remembered. "She told Director Doug she opened it a few minutes before noon."

"So the pumpkin smasher snuck into the tent

sometime between eleven and noon," Joe said, writing the timeline in his clue book.

"Now we have to figure out who," Frank said with a frown. "What creep would want to ruin a painted-pumpkin contest?"

Creep? The word made Joe's eyes light up. "Creep is Adam Ackerman's middle name!" he said.

"I thought it was Bradley," said Frank.

Joe rolled his eyes. "Seriously, though." he said. "I saw the zombies carrying long thingamajigs while they were running somewhere. They were heading in the direction of the Boo-seum, too!"

"Adam said they had 'that thing' to do," Frank said. "Maybe that thing was to smash pumpkins."

Joe wrote the word *Suspects*. Underneath he wrote: *Adam, Seth, and Tony.*

"Who else would smash the pumpkins," Frank asked, "and why?"

"Maybe someone didn't want the contest to happen," said Joe. "So he or she ended the whole thing with a splat!"

"Splat—as in Oliver Splathall!" Frank exclaimed.

"Oliver was mad that he couldn't enter his sculpture in the contest. His sculpture was the only one not smashed, too."

"Oliver must have come back for his tool bag," Joe pointed out. "He could have smashed the pumpkins while he was in the tent."

As Joe added Oliver's name to their suspect list, Frank heard a low, rumbling growl.

"What was that?" Frank asked. "Some bear or lion?"

"My stomach," Joe said, closing the book, "saying it's time for lunch!"

The boys headed to the zoo food court, also decorated for Halloween. There were rubber bats dangling from trees and skeleton arms reaching around the booths.

The pizza booth belonged to the Zamora family, who also owned the Pizza Palace, the coolest pizza place in Bayport. Frank and Joe went to school with Daisy Zamora and her six-year-old twin brothers, Matty and Scotty.

"Look!" Joe said. "Mr. and Mrs. Zamora are dressed up as vampires."

"They're selling pizzas named after animals, too," Frank said, reading the sign over their booth. "There's Panda Pepperoni, Marmoset Mushroom, and Cheetah Cheese!"

The first in line at the pizza booth was Aunt Trudy. Frank and Joe could hear her arguing with Mr. Zamora.

"You have no pizzas here for animals to enjoy!" Aunt Trudy said. "How about a pie with a nice lizard topping for the eagles or weasels?"

"Lizards on my pizzas?" Mr. Zamora exclaimed through plastic fangs. "No can do, lady. Next!"

Aunt Trudy frowned as she stepped out of line.

"Seriously, Aunt Trudy?" Joe asked. "Lizards on pizza sounds worse than anchovies."

"Oh, what difference does it make, Joe?" Aunt Trudy sighed. "So far I haven't had any luck finding fun things for animals to do today."

She pumped a fist in the air and said, "But I refuse to give up. If you'll excuse me, I'll be off to the Ape Habitat!"

"Why the Ape Habitat?" Frank asked.

"Gorillas have such nice long fingers," Aunt Trudy said excitedly. "Perfect for Halloween crafts!"

She walked away. Joe turned to Frank and said, "Should we get pizza slices?"

"Let's eat tacos instead," said Frank. "The thought of lizard pizza grossed me out."

On their way to the taco stand, the brothers spotted three guys sitting around a table eating pizza. All three were dressed as zombies.

"Joe," Frank whispered. "It's Adam, Seth, and Tony!"

"That's not all I see," Joe whispered back. "Look under the table."

Frank did look and his eyes widened. Underneath the table were—

"Mallets!" he hissed. "Three big mallets!"

Joe nodded. Mallets were like big hammers. And the ones under the table were crazy big!

"We may not have crushed the Scaryoke contest, Frank," Joe said, glaring at the bullies, "but I think I know what crushed those pumpkins!"

Chapter 5

MUSH RUSH

Adam, Seth, and Tony were so busy eating that they didn't notice Frank and Joe a few feet away.

"That's what you saw them lugging on their shoulders," Frank told Joe. "I wonder if those mallets have pumpkin mush on them."

"You mean the gooey, seedy stuff inside the pumpkin?" Joe asked. "Why would that matter?"

"If the bullies used those to smash the pumpkins,"

Frank explained, "the mallets would be covered with mush!"

He nodded in the direction of the table. "That's why we have to get a closer look at those mallets, Joe."

"Are you crackers?" Joe squeaked. "How do we do that with the bullies sitting over them?"

"Someone has to get their attention while we check out the mallets," said Frank slowly, "But who?"

"Say 'cheese'!" a high-pitched voice shouted.

"Extra cheese with pepperoni!" another voice exclaimed.

Frank and Joe whirled around. Standing behind them were the six-year-old Zamora twins, Matty and Scotty. They both wore vampire capes and had their hair slicked back.

"What are you doing here?" Joe asked.

Scotty lifted a phone and said, "What does it look like we're doing? We're taking pictures with our mom's phone."

"We're taking pictures of neat Halloween costumes like yours," Matty went on. "As long as we stay near the pizza stand and out of trouble."

"Good luck," Joe muttered.

But Frank was smiling with an idea. . . .

"Pictures, huh?" he said, pointing to Adam and his friends. "Why don't you take pictures of those zombies over there?"

Joe smiled as he realized Frank's plan. "Yeah!" he agreed. "They've got to be the best costumes at the Boo!"

Matty and Scotty looked at Adam, Seth, and Tony, then shook their heads.

"Nah," said Matty.

"Too scary," Scotty said.

"Exactly!" Joe said quickly. "You can use the picture to scare your sister Daisy!"

Frank shot Joe a look. Nothing scared nine-year-old Daisy Zamora. But the twins were already high-fiving.

"Let's take the zombies' picture and scare Daisy!" Scotty snickered.

"Wait," Frank told the twins. "Be sure you take lots of pictures without stopping in between."

"The more the better—I mean scarier!" said Joe. "And make sure they stand away from the table and face the other way."

"Why?" Scotty asked.

"Um . . . the light is better?" Joe guessed.

Matty and Scotty made their way to the bullies' table. Frank and Joe hid behind a tall trash can, peeking out to watch.

"While Matty and Scotty take pictures," Frank said, "we check out those mallets for pumpkin mush."

The brothers could hear Matty ask, "Can we take pictures of your zombie costumes?"

"How do you know they're costumes?" Seth guffawed.

But Adam pointed to the twins and said, "Wait a minute. Don't your mom and dad run the pizza stand where we just bought slices?"

"Yeah, so?" Matty and Scotty said in unison.

"So," Adam said slowly, "we'll let you take our picture in exchange for a jumbo pie with meatballs."

"We thought zombies ate brains!" Matty snapped.

But Scotty folded his arms across his chest. "We'll trade you six garlic knots instead," he said. "Take it or leave it."

After mumbling to his friends, Adam nodded and said, "Deal."

"Yes!" Joe cheered under his breath.

It was all systems go as the Zamora twins directed the zombies to stand with their backs to the table. When they were busy posing and growling for the camera, Frank and Joe rushed toward the mallets.

The brothers were inches away from the table

when they heard Matty say, "This came out awesome! Want to see it?"

Frank and Joe froze in their tracks as the bullies checked out the shot. Would they see the Hardys in the picture sneaking over to the table? Their answer came as Adam shouted, "Hey! Two jerks just photobombed us!"

The brothers gulped as Adam spun around.

"And I know who they are!" he said angrily. "Hardys!"

Chapter 6

ZOOMING ZOMBIE

"Did you photobomb us," Adam demanded, "or were you sneaking up on us?"

"Um . . . neither!" Joe blurted. "A meatball from my hero sandwich rolled under your table. Anyone see it?"

Adam picked up one of the mallets and said, "All I see is this!"

Seth and Tony sat down to finish their pizza. But Adam chased Frank and Joe as they began to run.

"Hey!" Matty called after him. "Don't you want your garlic knots?"

The brothers ran like the wind through the food court. Joe looked over his shoulder and called, "What's worse than being chased by a zombie, Frank?"

"What?" Frank called back.

"Being chased by a zombie swinging a mallet!" Joe shouted. "Run for it!"

Picking up speed, the brothers raced past one of the trick-or-treat stations. Joe bumped into a boy carrying gumballs. The gumballs spilled out of his hands and rolled in Adam's direction!

"Ahh!" Adam shouted as he tripped and stumbled over the rolling candies.

The gumballs slowed Adam down, but the brothers kept on running. Frank pointed to a fake cemetery in the near distance. "In there!" he called to Joe.

The brothers glanced back to see Adam charging toward the cemetery too. To escape him, they leaped over foam-rubber tombstones. A zookeeper wearing

a black cape and a real raven on his shoulder shouted, "Hey! No jumping over the tombstones. Snake around them instead!"

"Snake around, snake around!" the raven squawked. *"Kraa!"*

Snake? Joe's eyes lit up. *That's it!*

He turned to the zookeeper and asked, "Where's the Reptile House, please?"

The zookeeper pointed to a small house behind the fake cemetery. "Right over there," he said.

"Walk, don't run, walk, don't run," the raven screeched. *"Kraa!"*

"Why the Reptile House?" asked Frank.

"You'll see," Joe said.

Adam was about ten feet behind them as the brothers dashed into the Reptile House. It was dark inside, the only light coming from the snake tanks, eerily lit.

"Hardys!" Adam bellowed as he burst through the door. Stopping suddenly to look around, he began to shriek, "Snakes!"

A snake handler, a cobra wrapped around his neck, stepped out of the shadows. "Did someone say 'snakes'?" he chuckled. "Hope you're not . . . too *rattled*!"

The handler yanked a rope against the wall and *POOF!* Colorful rattlesnakes dropped from the ceiling, bouncing up and down over the brothers' heads!

"Cool!" Joe exclaimed.

Other kids in the Reptile House laughed and shouted happily. Everyone knew the snakes were fake. Everyone except Adam. Dropping his mallet,

he charged out the same door he'd come in, scream-
ing all the way!

"Adam really is scared of snakes!" Joe laughed.
"My plan worked. Right, Frank? . . . Frank?"

He turned to see Frank watching the mallet
that Adam had dropped. The big, heavy mallet was
bouncing across the floor!

Frank picked up the mallet, which wasn't
heavy at all. It was as light as a feather. Soft and
squishy, too!

"This mallet is made out of sponge!" said Frank,
giving it a squeeze. "It wouldn't smash a snowball!"

"Guess they didn't smash the pumpkins, then. Hey,
I wonder where Adam got it," Joe said. "The bullies
didn't have mallets when we first saw them in the zoo."

After a quick look at some real snakes, the brothers left the Reptile House. The exit door led outside
to a row of carnival games.

The game with the longest line of kids was the
Whack-a-Monster game. Kids seemed to have a blast
whacking costumed zookeepers with the squishy
mallets!

Frank and Joe walked over to the teenage girl working at the game. When they showed her Adam's mallet, she recognized it right away.

"That's our mallet," she said. "Three of them went missing after some creepy zombie kids played the game."

"Here's one," said Frank. "The others are with two zombies at the pizza stand."

"Thanks!" she said, taking the mallet.

The brothers played a quick game of Whack-a-Monster. Joe won a stuffed iguana but gave it to the kid whose gumballs he'd knocked down.

As the brothers walked through the zoo, Frank said, "So that's what Adam told Seth and Tony they had to do. Steal mallets from the Whack-a-Monster game."

Joe was about to cross Adam's name off the suspect list when he had second thoughts.

"Adam, Seth, and Tony are multitasking bullies," Joe said. "Maybe they took the mallets and smashed the pumpkins some other way—like picking them up and dropping them!"

Frank shook his head. "No. I was thinking about it, and I realized that smashing pumpkins is messy work," he said. "Their costumes would have been covered with pumpkin mush."

Joe's eyes widened as he said, "You mean . . . like that?"

Frank looked to see where Joe was pointing. Signing pictures of himself was Victor the Constrictor. But the strongman looked different from before. His bulging muscular arms and chest were dripping with orange ooze!

"Wow, Joe," Frank whispered. "Maybe Victor can smash pumpkins after all."

"Yeah," Joe whispered back. "The painted pumpkins in the Boo-seum tent!"

DUPER-HERO

Frank could see that Victor was covered with orange mush, but was it pumpkin mush?

"Why would Victor want to ruin a pumpkin-painting contest?" asked Frank. "He's such a cool dude."

"Victor couldn't smash the pumpkin in his show," Joe said. "Maybe smashing a bunch of pumpkins would prove he was still strong."

Frank remembered something else. "Some kids

yelled out stuff that wasn't cool," he said. "Victor said he'd show them who was the champ."

"Smashing painted pumpkins wouldn't make Victor a champ," Joe said angrily. "It would make him guilty as charged!"

"Not so fast, Joe," Frank said. "Dad always says, never accuse a suspect until you have solid proof."

"Right," Joe sighed.

Their dad, Fenton Hardy, was a private investigator in Bayport. When it came to mysteries, he knew the drill. Their mom, Laura, was a real-estate agent—so she knew the neighborhood!

"But should we still write Victor's name in the clue book?" asked Joe.

"Sure," said Frank. "Put him on our suspect list. Oh, and while you're at it, cross off Adam and his friends."

"What do we do next?" asked Joe. "Ask Victor some questions?"

The brothers turned to look at Victor. The Constrictor's enormous muscles swelled like balloons as he signed autographs.

"Um . . . why don't we look for clues first?" Frank gulped.

Joe watched as Victor signed a comic book for a fan. "Frank, he's not wearing his Victor the Constrictor gloves."

"Why would he?" asked Frank. "He's signing autographs."

"Sure, but when he smashes stuff, he wears reptile-claw gloves," Joe explained. "If he smashed those painted pumpkins, his gloves would be splattered with mush too."

"Then we have to look for Victor's gloves," Frank said. "Where do we start?"

"The hot dog stand," Joe declared.

"The hot dog stand?" cried Frank. "For Victor's gloves?"

"For lunch!" Joe said. "We haven't eaten yet, remember?"

Frank and Joe left Victor and his fans to look for the hot dog stand. They found it next to the zoo's giraffe pen.

A man in a hairy werewolf mask stood behind the counter. "What'll it be, guys?" he asked.

"One hot dog with mustard and relish, please," Frank told him. "And a bottle of water."

"I'll have a hot dog with extra ketchup and water, too," Joe said, before quickly adding, "Please."

As the werewolf ripped opened a package of frankfurter buns, the brothers turned toward the giraffe pen. Kids gazed up at long giraffe necks bobbing over the fence. But what stood next to the giraffe pen was what caught the brothers' eyes. It was a trailer painted with a snakeskin design.

"Neat trailer!" Joe said, pointing to it. "Is that another Reptile House?"

The werewolf handed over the hot dogs and water bottles. "That's not a reptile house, guys," he told the boys. "That's Victor the Constrictor's trailer. He uses it to travel to all his shows."

"Victor the Constrictor's trailer?" Frank asked excitedly. "Thanks for the tip—and the hot dogs."

"We'll try not to wolf them down!" Joe joked.

The werewolf rolled his eyes. "Everyone's a comedian on Halloween," he sighed.

As they walked away from the hot dog stand, Joe said, "Now we know where to look for Victor's gloves. Are we lucky or what?"

"It depends," Frank replied. "What if the door is locked?"

Joe pointed to an open window on the side of the trailer. "There's always another way!" he said.

Frank ate his lunch on their way to the trailer. Joe was still eating his as they approached the door.

"Be careful not to drip ketchup in Victor's trailer," said Frank. "Or we'll be toast!"

"More like applesauce with someone like Victor," Joe said with a shudder. He tried the door and it swung open. The brothers slipped into the trailer, closing the door behind them. But when they turned around—

"Whoa!" Joe cried.

Victor was standing right in front of them! Or was he?

"It's a cardboard cutout of Victor," Frank declared. He knocked on the cardboard and said, "See?"

Joe breathed a sigh of relief. "Let's look for those gloves, Frank," he said. "Before the real Victor gets back."

The brothers searched the trailer. They found snack foods, a small TV, bins of autographed pictures—but no reptile-claw gloves!

Frank was about to open a cabinet when they heard Victor's voice outside the trailer.

"I'm going inside to change, Doug," Victor was saying. "I'm still covered with pumpkin guts!"

"Okay, Vic," Director Doug's voice said.

Joe turned to Frank, his eyes wide. "Did you hear what he said?" he whispered. "He's covered with pumpkin guts!"

"He's coming back, too!" Frank said. "We have to hide!"

The brothers dashed behind the cardboard cutout of Victor. The cutout showed the star with both hands planted on his hips. The brothers peeked through the arms to watch Victor step into the trailer.

Humming the theme song from his latest movie, Victor reached down to peel off his muscles and tattoos. Underneath the inflated muscle shirt was a much scrawnier Victor, wearing a baggy T-shirt!

Victor tossed the pumpkin-splattered muscle shirt into a hamper. Then he opened the cabinet and pulled out a clean one.

While Victor put on his new muscle shirt, Joe whispered to Frank, "Did you see that? Victor the Constrictor is a fake!"

"Shhh!" Frank hissed. "Fake or not, we still don't want him finding us here."

Suddenly—*SLURP!*

Joe turned to see a giant tongue licking ketchup off his hot dog. Glancing up, he saw a giant giraffe's head sticking through the open window!

"Frank, Frank, Frank," Joe squeaked. "A giraffe is eating my . . . frank!"

LICK-OR-TREAT

Joe tried not to yell as the giraffe tasted his lunch. But when its huge tongue began licking his hair—

"Ahhh!" Joe shouted, dropping the hot dog. "Giraffe attack!"

Pulling himself away from the window, he knocked against the cardboard cutout. It tipped to the floor with a *THUMP*—revealing Frank and Joe.

Victor stared at the brothers. "Well," he chuckled. "If it isn't Dr. Frankenstein and his monster."

⇆ 57

"Um . . . hi," said Frank.

"What are you guys doing in here?" Victor asked with a small smile. "If you want an autograph or a selfie, just ask."

With licked-up hair, Joe turned toward the window. He pointed and said, "That giraffe up there was—"

Joe stopped midsentence. The giraffe's head was no longer at the window. . . . Awkward!

Frank decided to tell Victor the truth. "The painted pumpkins in the Boo-seum were smashed to slither-eens," he said bravely.

"You were covered with pumpkin mush," Joe added. "Where would that come from if you weren't smashing pumpkins?"

"From eating pumpkins," Victor replied.

"Eating pumpkins?" Joe repeated.

"I was in the pumpkin-pie-eating contest," explained Victor. "If I couldn't crush a pumpkin in my show, I was set on crushing the contest. And I did."

Joe looked around the trailer. "If you won the

pumpkin-pie-eating contest, where's your trophy?" he asked.

"I gave it to the runner-up," Victor said. "A kid who brought his own can of whipped cream. I never saw anyone else eat that much pie!"

"Was the kid's name Chet?" Frank asked.

"That's the guy!" replied Victor. While he propped up his fallen cardboard cutout, the brothers whispered to each other.

"Wasn't the pumpkin-pie-eating contest the same time as Scaryoke?" Joe asked.

"Yeah," said Frank. "That's why Chet couldn't come to cheer us on."

"So Victor was busy gulping down pumpkins at the time of the crime," Joe said. "Not smashing them!"

"How do we know Victor is telling us the truth?" Frank asked.

"Watch this!" Joe whispered. He turned to the strongman and asked, "Excuse me, Victor—but are your muscles real?"

Victor turned to stare at Joe. "Real?"

Frank shot Joe a puzzled look. Didn't they already know his muscles were bogus?

But Victor smiled and said, "Can you guys keep a secret?"

"Sure," Frank and Joe said together.

"Good," said Victor, pretending to flex his muscles, "because this whole Constrictor suit is really a costume."

He pressed his hands together. "All those things I crush in movies and on TV are phony too," he said. "They're specially made to smash easily."

"Wow," Joe said under his breath.

"Then how come you couldn't smash that pumpkin in your show?" Frank asked Victor.

"The zoo goofed," Victor sighed. "They put out a real pumpkin instead of one of my smashable props!"

Joe smiled at Frank. Victor was honest about his muscles and strength. He had to be honest about the pumpkin-pie-eating contest too!

"Thanks, Victor," Frank said. "Your secret is safe with us."

"I'll tell you a secret too, Victor," said Joe.

"Oh, yeah?" Victor asked. "What?"

"A giraffe really did try to eat my hot dog!" Joe said. "But we'll clean up the mess."

The brothers wiped splattered ketchup from the floor and tossed out the giraffe-licked hot dog. They then left the trailer, happy that their favorite hero wasn't the pumpkin smasher.

Joe crossed Victor's name off the suspect list. "We still don't have a *who* or *why*," he said, "and Oliver Splathall is our only suspect left."

"Where do you think he is?" asked Frank.

"Maybe he went back to the Boo-seum for his grasshopper sculpture," Joe said.

"Then that's where we're going too," Frank said.

"But first we better stop by the hot dog stand again," said Joe.

Frank chuckled. "Better eat it quickly this time."

On their way to the Boo-seum, the brothers passed the petting zoo. The two junior zookeepers were busy hosing down the animals, scrubbing them with soapy suds and patting them dry.

"Hey, JZ Squad!" Joe called to the zookeepers.

"I thought you guys washed the animals this morning."

Manuel and Stephanie stopped what they were doing to look at Frank and Joe.

"You can never wash animals too often!" Stephanie shouted.

"Clean animals are happy animals!" called Manuel.

"Oh yeah?" Joe chuckled. "Tell that to the hippos rolling in the mud!"

The two boys left the petting zoo and approached the Boo-seum tent. The flap used as an entrance had been pinned shut.

"How do we get inside now?" Frank asked.

With a smile, Joe said, "Follow me!"

Before Frank could stop him, Joe dropped to his knees. He slid under the thick canvas into the tent.

"Give me a break," Frank sighed before slipping under the tent too.

Once inside, the brothers saw Oliver's pumpkin sculpture still standing. But Joe's eyes were soon on the pumpkin shells on the sawdust ground.

"Hey, Frank," Joe said slowly. "What do you get when you smash a pumpkin?"

"How can you think of pumpkin riddles now?" Frank complained.

"It's not a riddle," Joe insisted. "What do you get when you open up a pumpkin? Like when we make jack-o'-lanterns with Dad."

Frank gave it some thought. "You get a ton of seeds and pulp . . . pretty much a mess."

"Exactly!" Joe declared. "So something important is missing from the tent."

"What?" asked Frank.

"The mush, Frank," Joe said with a smile. "Seedy, gooey pumpkin mush!"

Chapter 9

FOR THE BIRDS

Frank examined the smashed pumpkins. Joe was right. There were a lot of broken pumpkin shells but hardly any pumpkin mush.

"I don't get it," Frank said.

Just then the brothers heard loud chirps, squawks, and flapping noises outside the tent. "Sounds like birds," said Frank.

"A ton of birds!" Joe agreed. "Let's check it out."

He and Frank left the tent the same way they'd come in, sliding out from underneath. As they stood up, a flock of birds zoomed over their heads. The birds fluttered over to a woman sitting on a bench. She smiled as she scattered seeds on the ground.

"It's Aunt Trudy!" Joe said.

He and Joe could hear her call to the landing birds, "Come get your treats . . . or should I say *tweets*!"

"Hi, Aunt Trudy," said Frank as they walked over. "What are you doing?"

"I'm giving the birds a chance to trick-or-tweet," Aunt Trudy explained. "I filled a bag with pumpkin seeds, which are perfect for Halloween."

Frank and Joe looked down at the pumpkin seeds. Some were stuck together with stringy orange goop.

"They look pretty fresh," Frank said. "Where did you get them?"

"From Oliver—your sculptor friend," Aunt Trudy said as a bird landed on her shoulder. "He had a big plastic bag filled with pumpkin pulp and seeds."

"Oliver?" Joe exclaimed. He turned to Frank and said, "Oliver is one of our suspects, and he's packing pumpkin mush!"

"I wonder if it's the missing mush from the Boo-seum," Frank said.

"Mush? Boo-seum?" asked Aunt Trudy. "What are you boys talking about?"

"We'll explain later, Aunt Trudy," Frank promised.

"Can you tell us where Oliver is?" Joe asked their aunt. "Please?"

Aunt Trudy pulled her hand out of the seed bag. Another bird landed on her finger as she pointed. "I don't know exactly where Oliver is," she said. "But he was walking the same way as the costume parade."

Frank turned to see kids in costumes marching by. "Follow that parade!" he told Joe.

"Bye, Aunt Trudy!" Joe called back as they began to run. "And thanks!"

The brothers ran alongside kids dressed as ninjas, superheroes, cartoon characters, fairies, and mostly animals. Oliver was lugging a big plastic bag, which made him easy to spot.

"There he is," Joe told Frank.

Oliver broke out of the crowd. The brothers did too and followed. When Oliver was a good ten feet ahead of the brothers, Joe sniffed the air. "Whoa, Frank," he said. "What's that funky smell?"

Before the brothers could guess, Oliver walked to a big Dumpster. Standing next to it was a man holding a shovel. He spoke so loudly the brothers heard him loud and clear.

"Welcome to the Zoo Poo!" the man told Oliver. "I see you've got something there for me!"

Joe turned to Frank. "Did he just say Zoo Poo?"

Frank nodded. "I think it's the zoo's compost pile," he said. "We learned about it on a class trip."

The man pointed to Oliver's bag. "So are you donating animal waste to the Zoo Poo?" he asked. "Or vegetable waste?"

"One hundred percent pumpkin guts," said Oliver, handing over the bag. "Knock yourself out."

He dusted off his hands as he walked away.

"Frank, Oliver admitted he had pumpkin guts!" Joe said. "How do we find out where it's from?"

"Like this," Frank said. He cupped both hands around his mouth and shouted, "Hey, Oliver!"

Oliver stopped walking and turned around. When he saw the brothers, he replied, "What?"

"We just want to talk to you," Frank called. "About the pumpkin—"

"Can't!" Oliver cut in. "I've got to go!"

Oliver took off. Frank and Joe took off too—after Oliver. They chased him through the costume parade until he dashed straight into—

"The Haunted Woods!" Joe cried, and stopped in his tracks. "No way!"

Chapter

10

HAUNT JAUNT

"Let's go," Frank said, "or we'll lose Oliver!"

Joe shook his head at the entrance. The zoo's forest was said to be the scariest part of the Boo. It was filled with monsters, ghosts, and everything high on the creep-meter!

"I told you a million times," Joe said. "The Haunted Woods is a no-go!"

Frank groaned under his breath. "There's no such thing as ghosts, Joe!" he exclaimed.

"Oh, yeah?" Joe cried. He pointed to a figure at the entrance draped in a tattered shroud. "Tell that to Zombie Von Maggots over there!"

The zombie took a jerky step forward. "Come in, boys," she said. "We're all dying to meet you!"

"Ahh!" Joe yelled.

To get away from the zombie, Joe rocketed through the entrance. Frank thanked the monster, then ran into the Haunted Woods too.

The woods were thick with real and fake trees. It was dark even though it was the middle of the day. As the brothers searched for Oliver, they were surprised by rubber bats dropping from trees and zoo workers in monster costumes yelling, "Boo!" There were three witches stirring a cauldron of liquid, which turned out to be apple cider, and a path lined with scarecrows.

Frank and Joe followed the scarecrow path to a clearing. Sitting on the leaf-covered ground was a small crowd of kids. They all faced a tall object covered with a thick black cloth.

"What's underneath?" Joe wondered aloud.

A boy wearing a pointy wizard's hat suddenly stepped out from behind the object. The kids clapped their hands as the boy whipped off his cap and took a bow.

"It's Oliver!" Frank said.

Oliver put his hat back on and shouted, "Beware, beware—and be very, very scared. I hereby present to you—!"

Everyone watched as Oliver pulled at the cloth. It fluttered to the ground, revealing a scary-faced totem pole made of pumpkins. The five grimacing jack-o'-lanterns glowed from within.

"—the Towering Totem of Terror!"

Excited kids leaped to their feet. As they walked around the sculpture, oohing and aahing, the brothers approached Oliver.

"Why'd you run away from us, Oliver?" asked Frank.

"Because I was late for my big reveal," Oliver explained. "You know I never keep my fans waiting."

"Fans?" Joe asked. "Here at the zoo?"

"My fans are everywhere!" Oliver bragged.

Frank and Joe listened as the kids discussed Oliver's latest work of art.

"It's the perfect fusion of chaos and order!" one boy exclaimed.

"Oliver Splathall did it again," a girl squealed. "He created the perfect monster-piece!"

"Monster-piece!" Oliver chuckled to the brothers. "Remind me to write that on my blog."

Frank and Joe studied the pumpkins in the sculpture. They were hollow inside except for glowing LED lights.

"Is that where you got the pumpkin guts?" Frank asked Oliver. "The bag you donated to the Zoo Poo?"

Oliver nodded.

"I don't get it, Oliver," Joe said. "You already made a pumpkin sculpture shaped like a grasshopper. Why another one?"

"After I was bumped from the pumpkin-painting contest, Ms. Mitchell asked me to make a special sculpture for the Haunted Woods," Oliver explained, "something spookier than a grasshopper."

Oliver nodded at his tool bag, which was lying

under a tree at the edge of the clearing. "I went back to the tent for my pumpkin-carving tools, so I was good to go. After I was finished, I had so much mush I gave it to the Zoo Poo."

"And to our Aunt Trudy," Joe said with a smile. "The birds had a field day!"

Something Oliver had said jogged Frank's memory. "When you went back for your tools," he asked, "how did you get into the tent?"

"I untied the flap and went inside," Oliver said.

"Did you retie the flap on your way out?" asked Frank.

Oliver thought a minute, then said, "Oops. I think I forgot to. Why do you want to know?"

"The painted pumpkins in the Boo-seum were smashed," Frank explained. "The only pumpkins not destroyed were the ones in your sculpture."

"Why do you think that is, Oliver?" asked Joe.

"I don't think, I know!" Oliver said with a smile. Reaching into his tool bag, he pulled out a can labeled SCAT!

"Scat?" Joe asked. "What's that?"

"It's an all-natural spray to keep animals away," said Oliver. "It's got a lemony smell that most animals don't like."

"Why did you spray an animal repellent on your pumpkin sculpture?" Frank asked.

Oliver rolled his eyes and said, "Because we're in a zoo—duh! I didn't want to take any chances."

He put away his can of Scat, then returned to his fans.

"Oliver left the tent open," Frank said, "but I'm pretty sure he's not the pumpkin smasher."

"Me too," said Joe, crossing Oliver's name off the suspect list. "But now we have no more suspects."

Frank glanced over at Oliver's tool bag and the can of Scat peeking out. "I don't think the case is over yet, Joe," he said.

"What do you mean?" Joe asked, pointing to the page. "There's not one single person left on our suspect list."

Frank turned to Joe and smiled. "Who says the pumpkin smasher is a person?"

THE HARDY BOYS—and
YOU!

CAN YOU SOLVE THE MYSTERY OF THE SMASHED PUMPKINS?

Grab a piece of paper and write down your answers. Or turn the page to find out the answer to this boo-dunit!

1. Frank told Joe that maybe the pumpkin smasher was not a person. What do you think he meant by that?

2. Frank and Joe ruled out Adam Ackerman, Victor the Constrictor, and Oliver Splathall as the pumpkin smashers. Who else at the zoo might have smashed the painted pumpkins?

3. When working on a case, Frank and Joe come up with the five *Ws*: *who*, *what*, *where*, *when*, and *why*. Some detectives add a sixth word: how. How do you think the pumpkins in the Boo-seum got smashed?

Chapter

11

GOING GRAZE-y!

"What do you mean, Frank?" Joe asked. "If it's not a person, who is it?"

"Not who—what," Frank answered. "The only pumpkins left standing were the ones in Oliver's sculpture."

He pointed to Oliver's tool bag and said, "Oliver sprayed his sculpture with that stuff that keeps animals away!"

Joe's eyes popped wide open. "So the painted pumpkins were smashed by animals?" he asked.

"Maybe," Frank said.

"But animals don't run wild at the Bayport Zoo!" said Joe.

"Right," Frank agreed. "That's why we have to go back to the Boo-seum tent to look for more clues."

"Sure," Joe said, looking around. "But how do we get out of the Haunted Woods?"

"The same way we came in, I guess," said Frank.

Joe frowned, remembering the zombie, bats, and monsters. "I was afraid of that," he groaned. "Come on, let's go."

The brothers followed the scarecrow path out of the Haunted Woods and headed back to the Boo-seum. As they passed the petting zoo, Joe noticed something.

"The petting zoo is just a few feet away from the tent," Joe pointed out. "Close enough for the animals to get in there."

"But the JZ Squad is always in the petting zoo," Frank said. "How could the animals make a clean break without them seeing?"

Clean? Joe smiled as something clicked.

"The zookeepers washed the animals two times today," Joe said. "Maybe they were washing off pumpkin mush!"

"But why didn't they see the animals leave the petting zoo?" asked Frank. "And how did the animals leave?"

"Maybe the JZ Squad can tell us!" said Joe.

They walked over to the petting zoo. The closest zookeeper to the fence was Manuel, brushing fallen leaves from the llama's coat.

"Hey, dude," Joe called.

Manuel turned toward Joe. "What's up?"

"Not much," Joe said with a shrug. "Just wondering if any of the animals escaped the petting zoo today."

"Escaped?" Manuel scoffed. "The JZ Squad has their eyes on these animals at all times. Each one!"

Manuel lifted his arm to point to the animals. His sleeve moved, uncovering a rubber band on his wrist. It was the snake band the kids got at the Victor the Constrictor Show!

"Manuel's got the Victor the Constrictor wristband,"

Joe whispered. "That means he was at the show!"

"The show was at the same time the pumpkins were smashed," Frank murmured back. "The junior zookeepers said they weren't going to the show."

"What if they did?" Joe hissed. "And left the animals alone?"

"What are you guys whispering about?" Manuel asked.

"We were just talking about the Victor the Constrictor Show," Frank said quickly. "Too bad you guys missed it."

"Yeah!" Joe shouted over the fence. "Victor smashed a whole pumpkin between his hands—to slither-eens!"

Stephanie, who was helping a little kid feed a goat, turned around. "Wrong," she shouted back at the brothers. "Victor the Constrictor tried to smash the pumpkin, but he couldn't do it!"

"How would you know?" Joe asked.

"Because," Stephanie said. "We saw it when we were at the—"

She stopped midsentence to clap her hand over

her mouth. Her sleeve slipped up her arm to reveal a rubber snake band!

"So!" Joe declared. "You guys *were* at the Victor the Constrictor Show!"

"How do you know?" asked Stephanie, tugging her sleeve down to cover her band.

"It's all in the wrist!" Joe stated. "The proof, I mean."

Stephanie moved toward the fence. So did the llama.

"So what if we were all at the show?" Manuel asked. "What difference does it make?"

"The painted pumpkins were smashed at the same time as the Victor the Constrictor Show," Frank explained. "Maybe your animals broke into the Boo-seum tent while you were there."

"No way!" Manuel insisted. "Our animals were nowhere near any pumpkins."

Suddenly—

SPLAT! Another llama loogie was fired—landing on Frank's lab coat!

"Ugh!" Frank groaned. "Llama spit again!"

Joe watched the dripping blob and smiled. "More than spit this time, Frank," he said. "It's a clue!"

"What do you mean, a clue?" Frank asked.

"Notice the pumpkin seeds in the llama's spit," said Joe. "I may not be an expert on llamas, but I'd say he was feasting on pumpkins!"

"No wonder there was hardly any pumpkin mush in the tent," Frank stated. "The petting zoo animals did more than just smash pumpkins. They ate them."

Manuel folded his arms and said, "How do you know we don't feed our llama pumpkin?"

"You told us you only feed him those little brown things," Joe said. "If I were a llama, I'd escape too—for a better meal!"

The JZ Squad shrugged and shook their heads in defeat. Manuel turned to the brothers and said, "Okay, okay. We did go to see Victor the Constrictor."

Stephanie frowned at Manuel and said, "And one of us left the gate unlatched."

"It was an accident!" Manuel protested. "I remembered the gate while Victor was trying to squeeze that pumpkin."

"As we ran back to the petting zoo, we heard noises in the tent," explained Stephanie. "We peeked inside and saw our animals going wild!"

"The miniature horse, the pig, the goat, and the llama," Manuel sighed. "All stomping, smashing, and eating pumpkin guts and seeds!"

"We had a hard time getting them all back into the petting zoo," Stephanie said. "But nobody else saw the animals. Lucky for us, everyone was at the Victor the Constrictor Show."

Frank and Joe felt lucky too. They had just gotten

a confession from the JZ Squad. They also got their last *W. Who* . . . turned out to be the animals!

"You are going to tell Director Doug what happened," Frank told the junior zookeepers. "Right?"

"No way!" Manuel said, shaking his head. "We'd get kicked off the JZ Squad for leaving the animals alone in the pen."

"You have to tell Doug!" Joe insisted. "He said if they don't find the pumpkin smashers, there'll be no more Boo at the Zoo."

He pointed at the JZ Squad and added, "No more Boo . . . because of you!"

"No more Boo?" Stephanie gasped. "Say it's not true!"

"Okay, JZ Squad," said Manuel. "I just thought of something we have to do."

"What?" Stephanie asked.

Manuel frowned and said, "Fess up!"

Frank, Joe, and the two junior zookeepers found Director Doug in the Boo-seum, overseeing the pumpkin-mess cleanup. Aunt Trudy was also in the tent, taking a break from feeding the birds to help out.